DRAGON MASTERS

GUARDING ᴛʜᴇ INVISIBLE DRAGONS

WRITTEN BY

TRACEY WEST

ILLUSTRATED BY

MATT LOVERIDGE

BRANCHES

SCHOLASTIC INC.

DRAGON MASTERS
Read All the Adventures

More books coming soon!

TABLE OF CONTENTS

FOR KYLE AND SHAWN,

for bravely finding your way in the world and inspiring others
while you do it. — TW

The author would like to thank Kieron Scullington
for their help with this book.

Library of Congress Cataloging-in-Publication Data

Names: West, Tracey, 1965- author. Loveridge, Matt, illustrator.
Title: Guarding the invisible dragons / by Tracey West ; illustrated by Matt Loveridge.
Description: First edition. New York : Scholastic, Inc., 2022.
Series: Dragon masters ; 22 Audience: Ages 6-8 Audience: Grades 1-3
Summary: A nest of invisible baby dragons has been discovered in Queen
Sofia's castle so Drake, Worm, and Val, Carlos's cousin, must journey to
the dangerous Dove Island to find the parents and the fruit that keeps
the dragons' invisible powers.
Identifiers: LCCN 2021040218 (print) LCCN 2021040219 (ebook)
ISBN 9781338776904 (paperback) ISBN 9781338776911 (library binding)
Subjects: CYAC: Dragons—Fiction. Magic—Fiction. Fantasy. Adventure
and adventurers—Fiction. LCGFT: Fantasy fiction. Action and adventure fiction.
Classification: LCC PZ7.W51937 Gu 2022 (print) DDC [Fic]--dc23
LC record available at https://lccn.loc.gov/2021040218
LC ebook record available at https://lccn.loc.gov/2021040219

10 9 8 7 6 5 4 3   22 23 24 25 26

Printed in China   62

First edition, September 2022
Illustrated by Matt Loveridge
Edited by Katie Carella
Book design by Sarah Dvojack

TRAINING LALO

Drake shielded his eyes from the sun. He watched the baby Lightning Dragon swoop down from the sky in the Land of Aragon.

"Lalo, Bolt!" Carlos cried. The green Dragon Stone around his neck glowed brightly.

A lightning bolt shot from Lalo's right wing and hit the sand below.

Dragon Masters Drake and Carlos had been training with Lalo on the beach all morning. Drake's Earth Dragon, Worm, was watching. They'd found a spot near the cottage where Carlos lived with Diego, a wizard.

"Great job, Lalo!" Carlos called out.

"Whoo!" Drake cheered. "That was amazing!"

Drake still remembered the day when Lalo had hatched from an egg inside a pyramid. Brand-new and full of energy, the baby dragon had flown away. The Dragon Masters had searched many lands before they found him.

Then Griffith the wizard's Dragon Stone had chosen Carlos to be Lalo's Dragon Master. No Lightning Dragon is easy to control — especially a baby. But Carlos and Lalo had learned how to work together.

Drake and Worm had been on several adventures since then. They lived in Bracken Castle with Griffith and three other Dragon Masters. Now they were on vacation, visiting Carlos at the seaside.

Carlos walked over to Drake. "Thank you for helping today. Lalo has learned so much!"

Just then, a kid ran over to them. Val's wavy hair had a white streak in it, just like Carlos's did.

"Carlos! Drake! Abuela asked me to bring you this almond cake," Val said.

Drake grinned. "Your abuela knows it's my favorite."

Carlos's grandmother lived in a fishing village not far away. Carlos used to live with her. Then he moved into Diego's cottage to learn how to train Lalo. He visited his abuela every day, but she was a bit lonely. So Carlos's cousin, Val, had come from faraway to live with her.

"Abuela says I can stay for a few days and watch you train Lalo," Val said. "I had so much fun the last time I came."

"Great! Today, we're working on commands," Carlos said as Lalo landed next to him.

Val held out their hand to Lalo. The yellow dragon shot off tiny, happy sparks.

"You're so cute, Lalo!" Val said with a sigh. "I wish I had my own dragon."

"You can visit Lalo whenever you want," Carlos said.

Val nodded. "I know. But I still dream of becoming a Dragon Master one day. That's why I'm glad Diego lets me read his books about dragons. If the Dragon Stone ever chooses me, I'll be ready!"

Suddenly, the Dragon Stone that Drake wore around his neck glowed. He heard Worm's voice in his head.

Someone is coming.

A white horse appeared on the horizon, galloping toward them. The soldier on the horse wore a white-and-blue uniform. A braid streamed down her back.

The soldier brought the horse to a halt in front of them.

"Where is Diego?" she asked. "Queen Sofia demands his presence at the castle!"

"I'll get him!" Val ran to the wizard's cottage.

DRAGON TROUBLE

s Diego in trouble?" Carlos asked the soldier.

The soldier smiled. "No," she replied. "But there is trouble at the castle."

Drake looked at Carlos and the boys raised their eyebrows.

Then Val ran down to the beach, followed by Diego. An orange floated in front of the wizard, magically hovering in the air.

As Diego approached, the orange started bouncing on the horse's nose.

"So sorry," the wizard said. "I was in the middle of an animation spell. And I can't seem to stop it."

He pointed at the orange, and it floated back to him. "Now, how may I serve the queen?"

"A nest of baby dragons was" — the soldier began, but the orange floated over to her. It started spinning in front of her face — "was found in one of the castle towers."

"Baby dragons!" Drake cried. "What kind?"

"We're not sure, but they can turn invisible," the soldier replied. "And —"

She swatted at the orange, which zipped around her head.

"Can you please do something about this?" she asked.

Diego pointed at the orange and it flew back toward him. Val quickly grabbed it out of the air and tossed it to Lalo, who gobbled it down.

"Good thinking, kid," the soldier said. Then she turned to Diego. "Anyway, these baby dragons are causing trouble at the castle. And because you're an expert in baby dragons, the queen has called for you."

Diego nodded. "Carlos and I shall leave right away. Drake, you and Worm should return to Bracken."

"Do I have to leave?" Drake asked. "I'd love to help take care of invisible baby dragons!"

Val's eyes lit up. "Can I come, too? You're going to need help."

"Excellent! There is much I can teach you both!" Diego said. "Drake, please ask Worm to transport us all to the castle."

"Magical dragon transport?" the soldier asked. "Do you have room for two more?"

"Sure," Drake said. "We just —"

"Lalo!" Carlos yelled, interrupting Drake.

The Lightning Dragon zoomed up into the air and began to spin and loop. He moved so fast he looked like a yellow blur.

"Oh no!" Val cried. "The orange! It's making Lalo fly out of control!"

QUEEN SOFIA

Carlos's Dragon Stone glowed. "Lalo, cough!"

The dragon coughed, and the orange popped out of his mouth and landed in the sand.

Diego pointed his magic wand at the fruit. "Orange, orange you must stay. No more moving around today!" he chanted.

The orange stayed put.

"Wonderful!" Diego said. "Let us be on our way!"

Everyone made sure they were linked to Worm. The Earth Dragon glowed green. A bright light flashed, and the whole group transported in an instant.

"Whoa! That was fast!" the soldier said. "Follow me, everyone!"

They had landed outside Queen Sofia's castle in the royal city of Ursa. The castle's white towers gleamed brightly in the sunlight. Blue-gray roof tiles topped the towers.

The soldier climbed down from her horse and led them through the main entrance into the Great Hall. A long table stretched from one end of the room to the other.

Queen Sofia stood at the head of the table. She wore a blue-and-red gown with gold trim. A white scarf covered her head, topped by a golden crown.

"Diego, my royal wizard! Thank you for coming so quickly," the queen said. "And I see you've brought helpers."

The wizard bowed, and so did Drake, Carlos, and Val. Worm lowered his head, and Lalo followed Worm's lead.

Then Diego introduced eveyone.

"We hear you've found a nest of Invisible Dragons, Your Majesty," he said. "Babies."

"Indeed we have," the queen replied. "They are cute when I can see them, but they are causing too much trouble. Now please, sit and eat. Believe me, you will need the energy!"

They sat at the big table. Queen Sofia clapped her hands and servants appeared, carrying bowls of food. Drake's mouth watered as they filled his plate with fruits, vegetables, cheeses, and bread.

"It's a feast!" Val said.

On Drake's other side, Carlos giggled. "This is definitely better than the magical mystery mush that Diego makes every day."

As they ate, Queen Sofia explained the problem . . .

"One of my guards discovered the dragons' nest about a week ago," she said. "A few days before that, strange things started happening. Chairs falling over. Food disappearing. We thought we had ghosts!"

"That is a logical guess," Diego agreed.

"Then I saw one of the dragons appear and disappear right in front of me," Queen Sofia continued. "Their invisibility powers might explain why we have never seen their parents. But there is no sign of a mother or father dragon. The babies keep sneaking into the castle kitchen for food."

"Poor babies!" Val cried. "They must be hungry and scared on their own."

Queen Sofia nodded. "This is why I need your help," she said.

Suddenly, a bowl of figs in front of Drake floated up off the table. The figs vanished into thin air, one by one.

Drake's mouth dropped open in surprise. "Did an Invisible Dragon just eat those figs?"

CHAPTER 4

THE DRAGONS' NEST

rake watched the last fig disappear.

Then a loud *buuurp!* came from the fig bowl.

The air shimmered, and a baby dragon appeared on top of the table!

The dragon was about the size of a large dog. Her scales were a mix of shiny purple and green.

The dragon sat up and rubbed her belly.

"Gotcha!" a guard yelled as he lunged for the baby dragon.

"Don't scare her!" Diego warned.

The dragon jumped off the table and ran to the nearest corner, shaking.

Val got up and slowly approached the dragon. Everyone else in the Great Hall got quiet. Val crouched down. "It's okay. Nobody is going to hurt you. We want to help you."

The dragon took a step toward Val. Then she scooted into Val's arms.

Val giggled and patted the baby dragon. "Everything's going to be all right."

Diego stood up. "Well done, Val!" he said. Then he bowed to Queen Sofia. "Thank you for this wonderful feast, but I must see to the baby dragons."

"Shall we get there magically?" she asked, standing up.

"Yes, my Queen," Diego replied, and took her hand.

"Meet us in the tower!" Diego told the others, and then . . . *poof!* He and the queen vanished in a sparkle of magical light.

Then Worm transported Drake, Carlos, Val, Lalo, and the baby dragon.

They landed on top of a wide, round tower. A giant nest of straw had been built against one part of the wall. Three castle guards were chasing after four more baby dragons, who were running and tumbling all over the tower.

When the dragons saw Worm and Lalo, they ran to them, excited. Three of them climbed onto Worm's back! The fourth ran toward Lalo, but jumped away when the Lightning Dragon threw off a nervous spark.

Diego made a high, chirping noise. The baby dragons — including the one with Val — all stopped what they were doing. Five heads turned toward the wizard, their eyes wide.

Diego chirped some more, and the five dragons sat on their hind legs and stared at him.

"Wow, that's amazing, Diego!" Drake said.

"It takes practice," Diego said. He chirped again, and the five baby dragons jumped into their nest.

Queen Sofia nodded. "Well done, Diego," she said. "Now, can you and your helpers find their parents?"

Drake stepped forward. "Your Majesty, I can ask Worm to help. He can try to communicate with the baby dragons," he said.

"Then let him try," the queen said.

Drake gave Worm the command.

A minute later, Drake heard Worm's voice in his head.

The baby dragons communicate with feelings, he said. *They are confused and a little frightened. And missing their parents. That is all I can sense.*

Drake told this news to the others.

Diego frowned. "I was afraid of that," he said.

He snapped his fingers, and a sack of books appeared. "I have many books about dragons from this part of the world. Perhaps we can find a clue about the behavior of Invisible Dragons."

Val looked through the sack and pulled out a book called *Rare Dragons of the Southern Lands*.

Val handed it to Diego. "Look in chapter four. I remember reading something about Invisible Dragons in here."

"Wow, Val, you've been studying more than I thought," Carlos said.

Diego paged through the book. "You're right, Val, here it is!" he said. He read silently for a moment, and then frowned.

"Oh dear!" Diego cried. "The parents of these baby dragons may be in danger!"

THE THIRD HORN

Diego, why do you think the baby dragons' parents might be in danger?" Drake wondered.

The wizard began to read aloud. "Invisible Dragons are not invisible all the time. They can become visible at will."

Val patted the head of the fig-eating baby dragon. "That's a pretty cool power, little one."

Diego tapped the page. "But in order to keep that ability, the baby dragons must eat the fruit of the magical Dragon Tree before their third horn sprouts. There is only one tree, and it grows on Dove Island."

Queen Sofia raised an eyebrow. "Dove Island is one of the most dangerous places in all of my queendom!"

"That's why I'm afraid for the parents. They must have gone to the island to find this fruit," Diego added.

"What makes the island so dangerous?" Drake asked the queen.

"Rushing rivers, steep cliffs, and wild weather," she replied. "Anyone who has tried to settle there has quickly given up."

Carlos looked at the wizard. "How much time do we have?"

Diego examined the nearest baby dragon. "I can feel a bump underneath the scales. The third horn could sprout at any time."

"I have a question," Val piped up. "Why would *both* parents leave the babies behind to get the fruit?"

"I do not know. And since they have not returned, I must guess they are both in grave danger," the wizard replied.

Just then, Drake saw one of the baby dragons teetering on top of the tower wall.

"Oh no!" Drake yelled.

CHAPTER 6

THE SEARCH BEGINS

Drake quickly grabbed the dragon and pulled him to safety.

"That was a close one," he said as the baby climbed back into the nest.

"Oh dear!" Diego cried. "It's clear that I must keep a sharp eye on these babies at all times."

"Then I will send a team to explore Dove Island," Queen Sofia said.

"Worm and I will go!" Drake said quickly. "Worm can search for the energy of the dragon parents."

"Lalo and I will go with you, Drake," Carlos said.

Diego glanced over at the baby dragons. All five had gathered around Lalo. They stared in wonder as the Lightning Dragon shot off sparks to entertain them.

"Carlos, I think you and Lalo will be more helpful to me here," Diego said.

"I really want to help these baby dragons," Val said, stepping forward. "I'd like to go with Drake."

"Yes, that's a good idea," Diego replied.

Queen Sofia frowned. "Shall I send soldiers with them? They are just children."

"Drake is a very skilled Dragon Master. Val is very clever," Diego replied. "And Worm is the most powerful dragon I have ever met. The three of them will be fine. They will find the missing dragons, I am sure of it."

The queen looked at Drake and Val. "Be careful," she warned. "Dove Island is not as peaceful as the bird it is named after."

"We will," Drake promised.

Diego gave Val a bag containing *Rare Dragons of the Southern Lands*. "This book may be helpful," he said.

The little dragon that Val had calmed earlier looked up at them and whined.

"Don't worry. We'll find your parents," Val promised.

Green light flashed as Worm transported Drake and Val to Dove Island.

A SURPRISE

Drake blinked in the bright sunlight. They had landed on a cliff overlooking the sea. A strong wind blew, whipping Drake's hair into his eyes. In the sky, beautiful pink doves rode the winds.

Val's eyes were wide. "This place isn't scary. It's beautiful!"

Drake gazed around. The rocky cliff made it impossible to get down to the beach. An overgrown, jungle-like forest grew behind them. It led to a range of tall mountains.

"It is beautiful, but not easy to get around," Drake remarked. "It's a good thing Worm has transporting powers. Worm, can you sense the baby dragons' parents?"

Worm closed his eyes.

No, he replied. *But I do sense another dragon. One that is right here with us.*

"Worm says there's a dragon with us!" Drake announced, and as he spoke, a baby dragon became visible right in front of them!

"Fig!" Val cried. "Did you hitch a ride with Worm?"

"Fig?" Drake asked.

"This is the dragon that ate the figs in the Great Hall," Val replied. "I can tell because all of the fins around her face are solid blue-green. The others have some purple in their fins."

Drake frowned. "I don't think we have time to bring her back to the castle now. We need to find her parents — and the fruit from the tree — before it's too late."

Val nodded. "Don't worry," they said. "I will keep a close eye on Fig. I'll keep Fig — wait, Fig!"

The baby dragon was running toward the cliff!

FOLLOW FIG!

Val ran after Fig and dove, grabbing the dragon by the tail just as she tumbled over the edge of the cliff. Drake and Worm caught up to them.

"Fig, be careful!" Val warned.

The baby dragon sniffed the air. She whined and looked over the cliff's edge.

Val's eyes got wide. "Do you think Fig is on the trail of her parents?"

Drake heard Worm's voice in his head.

Fig might be tracking her parents' scent. Or she could be connecting with their energy. Her connection with them is likely stronger than mine. I still cannot sense them at all.

"You're right, Val," Drake reported. "Worm thinks Fig might be tracking her parents. Let's see if she can lead us to them."

"I think she wants to go down there," Val said, pointing to the beach below.

"Luckily, we don't have to climb down," Drake said with a grin. "Worm, please take us there!"

Worm transported them down to the beach.

Instead of soft sand, slippery rocks made up the jagged shoreline. Fig broke away from Val and headed inland.

It wasn't easy to keep up with the fast little dragon. Val tripped on the rocks, and Drake helped them up.

Then Drake, Worm, and Val caught up to Fig on the bank of a swiftly moving stream.

Before they could stop her, Fig jumped into the water! The dragon paddled downstream.

"Fig!" Val cried.

Drake turned to Worm. "We need to catch up to Fig!"

You and Val should climb onto my back, Drake heard.

"Val, jump on Worm!" Drake instructed.

When they were both on his back, Worm slid into the water.

"I didn't know Earth Dragons could swim, Worm!" Drake said.

The current will carry me, Worm replied. He floated downstream like a big raft.

Val gripped Worm's neck and called out to the baby dragon, "Fig wait for us! You can't do this alone!"

Fig flipped onto her back and grinned at Val.

Val sighed. "What am I doing? I'm not a Dragon Master. Fig can't understand me!"

"I think Fig really likes you, Val," Drake said. "She knows you care about her."

"I hope so," Val said. "I love animals, and I think they like me, too. Abuela's chickens always follow me around. But — oh no!"

The sound of rushing water hit them. The stream had become a waterfall.

"CHIRP!" Fig cried out in alarm as the water carried her over the edge.

INTO THE MOUNTAIN

rake's stomach lurched as the waterfall pulled Worm down, too. He held on tightly!

Splash! Luckily, the waterfall wasn't very high. The three of them landed in a shallow pool of clear water.

"Where's Fig?" Val cried. "We need to find her!"

Drake looked down. "It's not deep," he said. "I don't think she's underwater."

They both tumbled off Worm's back. Drake stood up. The water reached his elbows. He looked around but didn't see the baby dragon anywhere.

"Maybe Fig turned invisible," Val guessed.

"Worm, can you sense Fig?" Drake asked.

But before Worm could reply, the little dragon became visible on the shore.

"Fig! I was so worried!" Val cried.

Val, Drake, and Worm climbed out of the water, dripping wet.

Val hugged the baby dragon. "How about we stick to the ground from now on, okay?"

Fig motioned with her head for Val to follow, and trotted along the bank of the stream.

Drake, Val, and Worm dried off as they followed Fig.

The stream led them to a wide, open area at the foot of a mountain. Rocks were scattered across the ground. Some were boulders as big as Worm, and others were the size of barrels.

The stream flowed through the rocky area and then entered the mountain through a cave-like opening.

Suddenly, Fig took off toward a big pile of rocks. The baby dragon sniffed the ground as she moved. Her tail wagged.

"Fig seems really excited," Val said. "Do you think her parents are near here?"

Drake looked at Worm. "Can you sense anything?"

Worm closed his eyes. *Yes! There is dragon energy here. Energy that is not Fig's.*

The three of them approached Fig, who was still sniffing around the large rock pile.

The air next to Fig began to shimmer with purple-and-green light. Drake gasped. A big dragon was taking shape in front of their eyes!

TRAPPED!

ig made a happy, chirping sound and ran to the big dragon.

That is Fig's mother, Worm told Drake.

"Val, the dragon is —" Drake began.

"— Fig's mother, right?" Val finished.

The mother dragon nuzzled Fig. She had the same purple-and-green scales as Fig, but she had three horns on top of her head instead of two. And two of her horns were long and curved.

"Worm, please ask Fig's mom what happened here," Drake said. "Where's Fig's dad?"

Worm closed his eyes. After a minute, Drake heard the reply.

Her name is Tana, Worm began. *She is relieved to know that her babies are safe. Tana needed a place to lay her eggs and found the castle tower. She says that she and Fig's father, Yeray, came to this island to get the fruit from the Dragon Tree. It is a task that requires two Invisible Dragons. They thought it would be a quick trip. But as they were following the stream, there was an avalanche.*

Drake looked at the rocks piled up all around them. "These rocks tumbled down the mountain when Fig's mom and dad were here!"

Val gasped.

Yeray is trapped under the rocks, Worm continued. *He is invisible now to save his energy.*

"Val, Fig's dad is trapped beneath these rocks," Drake explained.

"That's terrible!" Val cried. "Is he okay?"

Yeray lost energy when the rocks hit him, Worm continued. *But Tana has been bringing him water and food, hoping he would become strong again. Then she thought they could move the heavy rocks together.*

"He won't be trapped for long," Drake said. "Worm, please move those rocks using the power of your mind."

Worm's body glowed green. He closed his eyes again.

"Stand back, everyone!" Drake yelled.

The rocks in the pile shone with green light. One by one, they floated up and away from the pile. Tana, Fig, and Val all watched with wide eyes.

"Is Fig's dad free now?" Val asked.

As Val spoke, the shape of Fig's father appeared for a second, then faded away.

"*Chirp! Chirp!*" Fig cried.

He is free, but he is weak, Worm answered. *Tana must get the fruit from the Dragon Tree for the babies. Yeray cannot make the journey to the tree.*

"Can't you transport him there, Worm?" Drake asked.

No, Worm replied. *Only Invisible Dragons can get near the tree. Fig will have to go with Tana, but she is worried Fig is too young.*

Drake repeated this to Val.

"Hmmm," Val said. "Fig was brave and clever when she snuck her way onto this island. She's the one who led us to Tana and Yeray. I believe Fig can do it!"

"I do, too," Drake said. "Worm, please tell Tana not to worry about Fig."

A few seconds later, Drake heard Worm's voice in his head.

Tana agrees. We must get to the Dragon Tree at once!

THE DRAGON TREE

ana and Fig led the way to the Dragon Tree, staying visible so that Drake, Worm, and Val could see them. Still weak, Yeray stayed behind.

The two Invisible Dragons took the group to the opening in the mountain. At first, it was dark in the cave, and Drake shivered.

They walked for a few minutes and then the tunnel opened up into a large chamber.

Standing outside the edge of the tunnel, Drake saw a strange purple sky overhead. "This is weird," he said. "We're in the middle of the mountain, but it's like we're not."

Val's eyes sparkled. "I think it's a magical place. Can you see that light up ahead?"

A faint purple light rippled in front of them. Beyond the light, Drake could see a moat surrounding a round patch of land. Growing on the land was a single tree with a wide, gray trunk. Its branches grew straight up. Green leaves covered the very top of the tree. Purple fruits dangled from the branches.

Tana says that only invisible creatures can pass through the energy field, Worm explained. *We must wait here.*

Drake repeated Worm's words out loud.

Val knelt down. "Good luck," Val whispered to Fig.

Fig and her mother turned invisible. The energy field shimmered and a moment later, they reappeared on the other side. They walked up to the moat.

Splash! A large, purple fish jumped out of the water. It snapped at the dragons with a mouthful of sharp teeth.

Splash! Splash! Splash! Several more toothy fish jumped out of the water.

Drake frowned. "How are they going to get past those nasty fish?"

Tana will distract the fish, Worm told Drake. *Then Fig will jump across the moat and get five pieces of fruit from the tree. One for each baby.*

The mother dragon became invisible again. She picked up a branch from the bank of the moat and waved it over the water. The fish jumped up and tried to bite it.

Fig turned invisible. Then Drake saw her footprints in the dirt as she landed on the other side of the moat.

The baby dragon turned visible again and scrambled up the bumpy tree trunk. Then she shook the lowest branches of the tree. The purple fruit rained to the ground.

"Oh no, how is Fig going to carry the fruit?" Drake wondered.

The baby dragon stared at the fallen fruit for a minute. Then she carefully started stuffing the fruit into her mouth. Her cheeks puffed up.

"She's going to try to carry them all in her mouth," Val guessed.

Fig scrambled back to the moat. Still invisible, Tana waved the branch to distract the fish. Fig made a running start toward the moat.

"Wait, Fig, you forgot to turn invisible!" Val called out.

Fig soared over the moat. One of the fish flipped around and saw Fig. Then it leapt up toward the baby dragon!

A MAGICAL FRUIT

The large fish snapped at Fig with its sharp teeth.

Bop! Tana's purple-and-green tail became visible. It smacked the fish.

The fish splashed back into the water.

Fig landed safely on the other side of the moat.

Tana's tail became invisible again, and so did Fig. The energy field protecting the Dragon Tree shimmered. Then Fig and Tana appeared in front of Drake, Worm, and Val.

"You did it!" Val cried, running to hug Fig.

The baby dragon spat out five purple fruits.

Then Tana nudged Fig with her snout.

Fig gobbled one up. The little dragon's body began to glow.

The glow faded as the fruit's magic took hold. Fig smiled.

Now Fig will keep her ability to become visible whenever she wants to, Worm told Drake.

"We need to get these fruits back to the rest of Tana's babies, before their horns sprout!" Drake remembered.

Val stuffed the four remaining fruits into their bag.

Everyone hurried back through the tunnel to Yeray. The father dragon was faintly visible.

He is feeling stronger already, Worm told Drake.

"Good! Get ready to transport back to Queen Sofia's castle," Drake said.

Val pointed at Fig, frowning.

"Drake, look! There's a little bump in the middle of Fig's forehead," Val said. "If Fig's horn is starting to sprout —"

"— the other babies might be sprouting their third horns, too!" Drake cried. He touched Worm. "Worm, please transport us now. We've got to get this fruit to the other baby dragons before it's too late!"

A SAFE HOME

Worm transported Drake, Val, and the three Invisible Dragons back to Queen Sofia's castle. They landed beside the nest on top of the tower.

The four baby dragons were listening to Diego tell a story. Carlos sat in the nest with them. Lalo was perched on the tower wall, in case the babies tried to climb it again.

The baby dragons chirped happily when they saw Fig and their parents. They scrambled out of their nest and tumbled over one another in their excitement.

Tana and Yeray, who was fully visible now, lowered their heads. They nuzzled all of their babies. Drake looked at the little dragons' foreheads.

"No horns yet!" he told Val. "We got here in time."

Carlos climbed out of the nest, and Drake and Val ran to him and Diego.

"You found the parents!" Diego cried. "And the missing baby, too."

"That's Fig. She followed us to Dove Island," Drake explained. "We got the fruit from the Dragon Tree. Fig ate hers, but we need to feed the other babies right away!"

Diego made a high chirping sound, and Fig's four siblings turned their heads. Then they scampered to Diego and lined up in front of him.

"Good dragons," he said, and he fed the babies as Val handed him the fruits, one by one.

Just as Fig had done, the four baby dragons glowed brightly from the magic of the fruit.

At that moment, Queen Sofia arrived in the tower. Her eyes widened at the sight of Tana and Yeray.

The queen turned to Diego. "You were certainly right to trust Drake, Worm, and Val. Well done, all of you!"

"Thank you, Your Majesty," Drake and Val said together. They both bowed.

"I have prepared a home for these dragons on the castle grounds," the queen continued. "Please let this dragon family know they may live here as long as they like."

Drake heard Worm in his head.

Tana and Yeray are very grateful.

"The dragon parents say thank you," Drake reported.

Diego bowed to Queen Sofia. "You are so kind, dear Queen. May I have your leave to go back to my cottage? I will return shortly to check on the dragons."

"As you wish, wizard," the queen replied.

Diego turned to Drake, Carlos, and Val. "Say your good-byes to these Invisible Dragons. It is time for us all to head home."

Val squeezed Fig, and Drake saw a tear roll down Val's cheek.

"Oh, Fig, I'll miss you," Val said. "But you're going to be so happy here with your family."

Drake heard the heartbreak in Val's voice. *It's too bad Val isn't Fig's Dragon Master!* he thought.

CHAPTER 14

DIEGO'S IDEA

oof! Diego used magic to return to his cottage. Worm transported Drake, Val, Carlos, and Lalo there, too.

"That was quite an adventure!" Diego said.

Val frowned. "I miss Fig already."

"I understand," Drake said. "I make friends on every adventure I go on. It's never easy to say good-bye."

Carlos grinned. "But sometimes we get to say hello again, like when Drake comes to visit. And I'm sure we can help Diego when he checks on the dragons back at the castle."

Val gave a small smile. "I'd like that."

Then Val's eyes got wide. "Something is licking my arm!"

The air began to shimmer purple and green. Fig appeared.

"Fig! Did you hitch a ride with Worm again?" Val asked.

The little dragon ran in a circle around Val.

"I'm happy to see you, too. But you have to stop running away from your nest," Val scolded. "We'll get a message to the castle so your parents won't worry."

Diego stroked his beard. "Hmmm. I have a thought, but we will need to go to Bracken to find out if I am right. First, we all need some food and a good night's sleep. It's been a long day!"

The next morning, after breakfast, Worm transported everyone back to Bracken Castle.

A minute later, they all appeared in the Training Room.

Griffith came out of the Dragon Masters'
classroom.

"Drake! Worm! How good to see you again!
We've missed you," the wizard said.

Drake's friends Bo, Ana, and Rori followed
Griffith.

Drake introduced everyone. Then they all started talking at once.

"How was your trip?" Bo asked.

"Is this another baby dragon?" Rori asked, looking at Fig.

"And are you her Dragon Master?" Ana asked Val.

Val sighed. "I wish I was."

"That is why we are here," Diego explained. "Griffith, it is clear to me that Val and Fig have formed a very strong connection in a short amount of time."

Griffith nodded. "I understand. To my workshop, everyone!"

Worm and Lalo watched through the doorway as Griffith, Diego, and the others gathered in the wizard's workshop. Griffith opened up a wooden box carved with an image of a dragon. Inside glittered a large green stone.

"Dragon Stone, show me the Dragon Master of Fig the Invisible Dragon!" Griffith said.

The Dragon Stone instantly glowed with bright green light!

A PERFECT PAIR

he light from the Dragon Stone turned into a single beam. That beam shone right on Val! Their whole body lit up with the green light!

"Excellent!" Griffith cheered. "The Dragon Stone usually shows us a new Dragon Master. But Fig's Dragon Master is right here!"

Val's mouth opened in shock. "You mean . . . it's me? I'm Fig's Dragon Master?"

"Indeed you are!" Griffith said. "When a human and a dragon form a bond like the one you have, the Dragon Stone knows. And Fig can use a caring Dragon Master like you."

The light from the Dragon Stone faded.

Diego smiled. "I know you'll be an excellent Dragon Master, Val."

Griffith opened another box and took out a small piece of the Dragon Stone hanging on a gold chain. He slipped it around Val's neck.

Val's Dragon Stone immediately began to glow.

"I can hear Fig inside my head!" Val cried. "Not words but . . . feelings."

"The same thing happened when Lalo was just born," Carlos explained. "But now we understand each other's words."

Val closed their eyes. "Fig is . . . hungry!"

Laughing, Val hugged Fig. "I will take such good care of you, Fig! I promise."

Griffith looked at Diego. "Now Val just needs a wizard to learn from."

"Of course I'll do it! You don't need to hint," Diego said. "Carlos and Val are already cousins. Now they can train together."

"I'm excited, but . . . I can't leave Abuela all by herself," Val said.

"I think it's time Abuela came to live with us," Diego replied. "I'll just magic up another room on the cottage for her. She does make a wonderful almond cake."

Carlos and Val grinned at each other.

Diego turned to Drake. "Do you think Worm would mind getting us all back to Aragon?"

"No problem," Drake said, and he looked at his friends. "Be right back!"

"Meet us in the Valley of Clouds," Griffith said. "We'll have a welcome-home picnic."

In a flash, Worm transported Drake, Carlos, Val, Diego, Fig, and Lalo back to the wizard's cottage.

"Thanks for letting me have a vacation here," Drake told them all. "Maybe one day you can come for a nice, long visit in Bracken."

"Lalo and I would love that," Carlos replied.

"No vacation for me until I've completed some training!" Val said.

Drake and Worm said good-bye to everyone.

Then they transported back to the Valley of Clouds.

Their friends were there, staring up at the sky. They looked worried.

Normally, white clouds floated in a blue sky above the valley. But now, a strange darkness was creeping across the land.

Drake frowned. "Is it nighttime already? Those don't look like storm clouds."

It is not night. It is not a storm, Worm replied.
Something bad is coming...

TRACEY WEST is a *New York Times* bestselling children's book author. She hopes that every kid, just like Val, can imagine themselves being a Dragon Master. Tracey is the stepmom to three grown-up kids. She shares her home with her husband, dogs, chickens, and a garden full of worms. They live in the misty mountains of New York State, where it is easy to imagine dragons roaming free in the green hills.

MATT LOVERIDGE lives with his wife and kids in the mountains of Utah. Matt is a children's book illustrator and has illustrated for several different series. Matt loves drawing dragons and other, non-magical creatures. In his free time he enjoys hiking and being outdoors with his family, and walking his dog, which despite being smaller than a dragon eats just as much as one.

DRAGON MASTERS
GUARDING THE INVISIBLE DRAGONS

Questions and Activities

When the story begins, Val knows a lot about dragons. How does Val learn so much about dragons? And how does this knowledge come in handy? Reread pages 5 and 27.

Queen Sofia warns that "Dove Island is not as peaceful as the bird it is named after." Why does she say this? What are doves a sign of?

Dove Island is one of the most dangerous places in Aragon. List three dangerous things that Drake and Val encounter on the island.

Tana chooses to build a nest in the castle tower. In real life, birds look for high places to nest. Do some research! Why do birds choose to nest up high?

Fig has four siblings! What would you name the other baby Invisible Dragons? Name them and explain why you chose those names!